BEING US

BEING US

Perceiving God, A Radical View

Lewis Randa

Includes translations into the major
languages of the United Nations:
Spanish, French, Russian, Chinese, Arabic.

Charleston, SC
www.PalmettoPublishing.com

BEING US

Copyright © 2022 by Lewis Randa

All rights reserved.

Author photo by Michael Parks Randa

First Edition

Hardcover ISBN: 978-1-68515-678-7
Paperback ISBN: 978-1-68515-679-4
eBook ISBN: 978-1-68515-680-0

TABLE OF CONTENTS

Section One
BEING US

Perceiving God, A Radical View

Section Two
Translation Appendix

*Major Languages
of the United Nations*

"How much more personal can God get, if, in fact, the experience I am having, God is having — not in addition to, not with, not through, but having exactly as I am having, when I am having it —because we are one and the same in time and space?"

DEDICATION

*Being Us is dedicated
to uplifting the spirit of awareness
of God's presence in our lives.*

PREFACE

Being Us was written in plain, conversational language so its message would be available to readers of all ages. The formatting of the material and general layout are designed to pace the reader through incremental assimilation of perceptions that may be contrary to one's religious upbringing and understanding. This concise, unimposing book, breaks through the patriarchal, dualistic concept of deity, not from an esoteric, theological point of view, but simply, through a dream during a dark night of the soul. Were it not for religious teachings from the majority of faith traditions over time, the message in this book would be intuitively self-evident. This reflection, hopefully, will put a chink in the armor of dualistic thinking, especially when it comes to perceiving a personal God in your life.

Pay attention to your dreams, dear friends, for they can lead to an epiphany that is life changing. Thus, is the case with this dream I now share with you in book form – a dream that took my perception of God and turned it inside out. It is translated into the major languages of the United Nations for its message is global and its intent divine.

While on your path, keep your eyes open to that of God in everyone and everything around you. There is more of God in your life than you can possibly imagine - more than meets the eye, even once you've seen the forest through the trees.

Lewis M. Randa

Dreams can have the most amazing effect on people, but to be honest, I rarely remember dreams long enough to consider any of them all that important.

One dream, however, I cannot stop thinking about and it has changed the way I view reality. How long the substance of this dream will pervade my mind and spirit is anyone's guess. I hope it lasts a lifetime.

With each tragic and horrible bit of news these days, and there have been many, I have been struggling with the question that countless others struggle with as well, and that is; how could there be a "personal" God?

With all the suffering in the world —famine, poverty, indifference, violence, war and disease — how could a personal God allow these things to happen, given that God, supposedly, is in charge.

Free will is one thing, senseless tragedy another.
I have pretty much concluded, after considerable
reflection over time, that there being a personal God
is but a hopeful and comforting idea which I learned
in catechism.

But, however, in light of all the tragedy and suffering around us, this is seemingly not the case. Or, if there is a personal God who would allow these things to happen to anyone at any time, then I certainly am missing something.

Then one night, Christmas night, through a dream,
what I was missing was explained to me.

I retired following a wonderful Christmas day 2010 with my family. Our holiday ritual included the recitation of the prayers for peace of the major faith traditions in the interfaith chapel at The Peace Abbey. Though troubled by the recent tragic death of a friend of my daughter, I was at peace, at least with the principle that everyone and everything that exists is an expression or creation of a loving God.

What I was struggling with, however, was that this so-called loving God would permit such horrible things to happen so randomly in the world. No doubt, nearly everyone has had that thought cross their mind at some point, only to work through it until it had to be addressed again, under new and different and difficult circumstances.

What I failed to understand, until it was revealed to me in the dream, was that God, whom I questioned a personal relationship with, actually experiences what we experience — physically, emotionally and mentally, with each and every experience everywhere, at all times and that is why all things are allowed to happen. God isn't just allowing things to happen to us, God allows things to happen to itself.

The dream provided an awareness that whatever can occur in our earthly existence is worth occurring. It is worth occurring because, through these experiences, God comes to know itself by experiencing all the pain, just as we do - all the joy, just as we do - all the sorrow and grief, just as we do - and when we do.

And that, the dream conveyed, is because everything that exists *is God*. There is nothing that exists that isn't.

It seems that in the process of being born into a physical body, and succumbing to continuous phases of ego development, we become detached, not only from our connection with God,

but more accurately, the awareness that *we are God*, and everything around us *is God*, and every experience we are having (this bears repeating), fundamentally, *is God having the experience.*

That thought never occurred to me. I sensed that everything was in God's control in a macro-universal sense, but never came close to considering God as having my personal experiences.

That changes everything. I feel I now need to reread every important and meaningful text, scripture, poem, prayer and revisit every philosophy, ideology, theory and principle of life on which I have based my understanding. The dream was for me the mother lode of all paradigm shifts.

What God is on earth was clarified for me,
in intimate terms, through the dream.

I now recognize, more than ever, that surrendering one's ego is required to illuminate the awareness that there is a personal God to whom my physical body and personality give form.

How much more personal can God get, if, in fact, the experience I am having, God is having — not in addition to, not with, not through, but having exactly as I am having, when I am having it, because we are one and the same in time and space?

Within earthly existence, this oneness has confounded humanity in its search for God, as God is concealed within the ego framework of personhood.

As this was being communicated through the dream, a sense of profound peace and self-surrender enveloped me.

I found myself in an alert state of sleep with no images or backdrop that I can recall. I felt like I was being told the secret of the universe which, perhaps, others are aware of, but I certainly was not.

Prior to the dream, I understood each experience I had as me having alone. How could it be otherwise?

I was taught that God was *aware of all things,*
even my experiences. I was never taught, however, that
God *is all things,* and therefore *aware of all things*; and is
aware of all things, because God *is experiencing all things!*

———————— ● ————————

We think, because of our separation from what we really are, personal experience is ours alone. My dream told me otherwise. It was as though I saw God the next day in everyone and everything around me.

Now it seems the very question, "*is there a personal God?*"
is akin to a cell on my physical body questioning a
personal relationship with me because the cell is unable
to appreciate the relationship between us.

The relationship, of course, is so integral,
so one and the same, that it is indiscernible.

———————— ● ————————

While we can assume God is much more than what
is taking place in the cosmos, it is enough to know
that where God exists on Earth is as personal as each
beat of our heart, for we are the outward and visible
embodiment of Godhood.

We are the physical form, imbued with a concept of self, that at once denies we are God, while existing for the sole purpose of *God being us.*

And in being us, God experiences in the first person
the reality we create.

So, I awoke the next morning with a sense that what was explained to me in a dream now needs to be absorbed so I never again fall into thinking (from an earthly point of view),

that God is something other than everything and everyone, and then begin questioning whether or not he/she/it is personally involved or cares enough to prevent horrible things from happening.

Forgive the redundancy once more: If something can happen, no matter how horrific and unfair or wonderful and affirming, it is allowed to happen.

It is allowed to happen because God manifests itself
through us, and all of nature, in order to experience
everything that can happen (both the good and the
bad, in our terms, and everything in between),
and therefore, we and everything else are created
and exist for that end.

And because
it's God's experience,
it's our experience too,
not the other way around.

Thus, God couldn't be more personal, and as such, mystifyingly, doesn't seem to be personal at all. Or even exist for that matter.

Before the dream, none of this crossed my mind. Talk about not seeing the forest through the trees.

For years I have been drawn to the saying:
If you can't see God in all, you can't see God at all.

I never really understood it until now. Thanks to the dream, this saying awakens me to a *sacred awareness* that takes my breath away.

EPILOGUE

B*eing Us* is an awareness that I have cultivated since having the dream in 2010—it provided a shift in consciousness that has been nothing short of awe-inspiring, sacred, and life-changing. Recognizing God as oneself (and as others), versus viewing God as an unseen, external, creative force (separate from us), requires the evolving of one's spirit and a deepening of one's God/Soul connection through new spiritual insights, sensitivity and intuition. It opens a new way of being, through a whole new way of seeing. I now see clearly a world where there is nothing going on that isn't the wondrous reality of *God being us.*

Being Us is seeing, as one who sees, through the eyes of God.

Lewis M. Randa

Enlightenment is
when a wave
realizes it is
the Ocean.

- Thich Nhat Hanh

Being Us stone at The Pacifist Memorial in
Sherborn, Massachusetts.

ABOUT THE AUTHOR

Lewis Randa is a Quaker, pacifist, vegan, and social change activist. He founded The Life Experience School for children and adults with disabilities in 1972, The Peace Abbey, an interfaith Center for the study and practice of nonviolence in 1988, and The Pacifist Memorial, an international monument that commemorates the lives of peacemakers in 1994. His peace work has brought him to the far corners of the world -- from El Salvador to Belfast, Liverpool to Calcutta, Assisi to Guernica. Lewis and his wife Meg, with whom he administers these organizations, have three grown children, Christopher, Michael and Abigail, and a growing number of grandchildren. They live in the seaside town of Duxbury, Massachusetts.

TRANSLATION
APPENDIX

*Major Languages
of the United Nations*

SOMOS UNO (BEING US)
Percibir a Dios, una visión radical

«Somos uno» está dedicado a elevar el espíritu de conciencia y a comprender la presencia de Dios en nuestras vidas.

«¿Cómo podría Dios ser todavía más personal si lo que yo experimento, en realidad, lo experimenta él —no lo hace aparte, ni conmigo, ni a través de mí, sino que vive exactamente la misma experiencia que yo, en el mismo momento que yo— porque somos un mismo y único ser en el tiempo y el espacio?».

¿Alguna vez te has preguntado por qué ocurren cosas terribles? O, ¿te has cuestionado que haya un Dios personal? Tras la trágica muerte de un íntimo amigo de su hija, Lewis Randa tuvo un sueño transformador que alteró su visión sobre la existencia de Dios. En *Somos uno*, Lewis reflexiona acerca de lo que él describe como una noche oscura del alma y comparte una asombrosa revelación sobre el papel que tiene Dios en nuestras vidas, que difiere en gran medida de la narrativa que promueven las principales religiones del mundo. Lewis descubre puntos en común con el budismo y la filosofía oriental, y describe cómo abrazó la doctrina del panenteísmo. Mediante un relato revelador que invita a la reflexión, *Somos uno* lanza un mensaje inspirador que resultará atractivo para cualquiera que tenga una mentalidad abierta, una profunda curiosidad por la creación y la voluntad de superar el pensamiento dualista en pro de un sentido de unidad con respecto a Dios.

PREFACIO

Somos uno está escrito en un lenguaje sencillo y familiar para que su mensaje pueda llegar a lectores de cualquier edad. El formato del material y su estructura general se han diseñado para guiar al lector a través de la asimilación gradual de percepciones que pueden ser contrarias a su educación y sus conocimientos religiosos. Este libro, humilde y sucinto, se abre camino en el concepto dualista y patriarcal de deidad, no desde un punto de vista esotérico ni teológico, sino simplemente mediante un sueño acontecido durante una noche oscura del alma. Si no fuera por las enseñanzas religiosas de la mayoría de credos tradicionales que se han dado a lo largo del tiempo, el mensaje de este libro sería intuitivamente obvio. Con un poco de suerte, esta reflexión abrirá una grieta en el pensamiento dualista, en especial cuando se trate de percibir a un Dios personal en nuestras vidas.

Queridos amigos, prestad atención a los sueños, pues pueden llevaros a una epifanía transformadora. Este es el caso del sueño que voy a compartir con vosotros en forma de libro; un sueño que puso patas arriba la percepción que tenía de Dios. Se ha traducido a los idiomas principales de las Naciones Unidas porque su mensaje es global y su propósito, divino.

Mientras sigues tu camino, mantén los ojos abiertos a Dios en todos los seres y todas las cosas que te rodean. Dios está presente en tu vida más de lo que puedas imaginar, más de lo que salta a la vista, incluso tras apreciar el bosque entre los árboles.

Lewis M. Randa

Sobre el autor:
Lewis Randa es cuáquero, pacifista, vegano y activista por la transformación social. En 1972 fundó la escuela The Life Experience School para niños y adultos con discapacidad. Más tarde, en 1988, creó The Peace Abbey, un centro interconfesional para el estudio y la práctica de la no violencia y, en 1994, The Pacifist Memorial, un monumento internacional que conmemora la vida de quienes se dedican a promover la paz. Su trabajo por la paz le ha llevado a los rincones más remotos del planeta: de El Salvador a Belfast, de Liverpool a Calcuta y de Asís a Guernica. Él y su esposa Meg, junto con la que gestiona estas organizaciones, tienen tres hijos ya adultos, Christopher, Michael y Abigail, y un número creciente de nietos. Viven en Duxbury, una localidad costera de Massachusetts.

SOMOS UNO

Los sueños pueden tener un efecto de lo más sorprendente en las personas, pero, siendo honesto, rara vez los recuerdo el tiempo suficiente como para considerarlos importantes. Sin embargo, tuve un sueño en el que no puedo dejar de pensar y que ha cambiado mi visión de la realidad. El tiempo que la sustancia de este sueño impregnará mi mente y mi espíritu es una incógnita. Pero espero que sea el resto de mi vida.

Con cada una de las noticias trágicas y horribles que suceden en la actualidad —que no son pocas— he tratado de encontrar respuesta a la pregunta que les ronda la cabeza a muchísimas personas: ¿cómo es posible que haya un Dios «personal»?

Con todo el sufrimiento que existe en el mundo —hambre, pobreza, indiferencia, violencia, guerras y enfermedades—, ¿cómo podría permitir un Dios personal que todo esto sucediera si se supone que Dios es el responsable de todo?

El libre albedrío es una cosa; las desgracias sin sentido, otra. Tras mucho reflexionar a lo largo del tiempo, había llegado prácticamente a la conclusión de que la existencia de un Dios personal no es más que una idea esperanzadora y reconfortante que aprendí en catecismo. No obstante, a la luz de todas las tragedias y el sufrimiento que nos rodean, no parece que sea cierto. O, si existe un Dios personal que permite que le ocurran estas cosas a cualquiera en cualquier momento, sin duda hay algo que se me escapa.

Una noche, la noche de Navidad de 2010, recibí una explicación a aquello que no entendía a través de un sueño.

Me había retirado tras un maravilloso día de Navidad con mi familia. Nuestro ritual festivo incluía recitar las oraciones por la paz de las principales tradiciones religiosas en la capilla interconfesional The Peace Abbey. Aunque afligido por la trágica y reciente muerte de un amigo de mi hija, me sentía en paz, al menos con el dogma de que todos los seres y las cosas que existen son la expresión o creación de un Dios bondadoso.

Sin embargo, me encontraba luchando contra la idea de que este supuesto Dios bondadoso pudiera permitir que sucedieran cosas tan terribles de forma tan azarosa en el mundo. Sin duda, a casi todos nos ha rondado la cabeza este pensamiento en algún momento, solo de pasada, hasta tener que enfrentarlo de nuevo en circunstancias difíciles distintas.

Lo que no conseguía entender hasta que se me reveló en el sueño era que en realidad Dios, con el que me cuestioné tener una relación personal, vive las experiencias que nosotros vivimos —física, emocional y mentalmente, todas y cada una de ellas, en cualquier lugar, todo el tiempo— y por eso todo puede suceder. Dios no solo deja que nos pasen cosas a nosotros; Dios permite que las cosas le pasen a él.

El sueño me hizo darme cuenta de que lo que sea que nos pueda ocurrir durante nuestra existencia terrenal vale la pena que ocurra —ya sea algo alegre o trágico— porque, a través de estas experiencias, Dios se llega a conocer a sí mismo al sentir el dolor igual que nosotros; la alegría igual que nosotros; la tristeza y la pena igual que nosotros, y al mismo tiempo que nosotros. Y el motivo, según me transmitió el sueño, es que todo lo que existe *es* Dios. No hay nada que exista y no lo sea.

Parece que, en el proceso de nacer en un cuerpo físico y sucumbir a las continuas fases de desarrollo del ego, no solo nos desconectamos de Dios sino que, más bien, nos desprendemos de la conciencia de que *nosotros somos Dios*, de que todo lo que nos rodea *es Dios* y de que cada experiencia que vivimos (esto vale la pena repetirlo), fundamentalmente, *la vive Dios*.

Nunca se me había ocurrido ese pensamiento. Intuía que Dios lo tenía todo bajo control en un sentido macrouniversal, pero nunca había llegado a considerar que Dios vivía mis experiencias personales. Eso lo cambia todo. Siento que ahora tengo que releer cada texto, escritura, poema u oración importante y valioso, y repasar cada principio vital, teoría, ideología o doctrina filosófica en los que he basado mi entendimiento. El sueño fue para mí la fuente principal de todos los cambios de paradigma.

A través de ese sueño, de forma íntima, se esclareció para mí el sentido de Dios en la tierra. Ahora reconozco, más que nunca, que es necesario abandonar el ego para iluminar la conciencia de que hay un Dios personal al que mi cuerpo físico y mi personalidad dan forma. ¿Cómo podría Dios ser todavía más personal si lo que yo experimento, en realidad, lo experimenta él —no lo hace aparte, ni conmigo, ni a través de mí, sino que vive exactamente la misma experiencia que yo, en el mismo momento que yo— porque somos un mismo y único ser en el tiempo y el espacio?

En la existencia terrenal esta unidad ha confundido a la humanidad en su búsqueda de Dios, pues Dios se oculta dentro del marco del ego de la personalidad. A medida que recibía este mensaje a través del sueño, me envolvía un sentimiento de profunda paz y autorrendición. Me encontré a mí mismo en un estado de alerta del sueño sin imágenes ni telón de fondo que poder recordar. Sentí que me estaban contando el secreto del universo que quizás otros ya conocían, pero del que yo, desde luego, no era consciente

Antes del sueño, cada experiencia que vivía la entendía como vivida en soledad. ¿Cómo iba a entenderlo de otro modo? Me enseñaron que Dios es *omnisciente*, lo conoce todo, incluso mis experiencias. Sin embargo, nunca me enseñaron que Dios *es* todo y, por tanto, *lo conoce todo*; y Dios lo *conoce* todo porque *lo experimenta* todo. Creemos que, por nuestra separación de lo que realmente somos, la experiencia personal es solo nuestra. En mi sueño descubrí lo contrario. Fue como si al día siguiente viera a Dios en todas las personas y todas las cosas que me rodeaban.

Ahora me parece que la pregunta «¿existe un Dios personal?» equivale a que una célula de mi cuerpo físico se cuestione su relación personal conmigo porque dicha célula no sea capaz de apreciar la relación que existe entre nosotros. Naturalmente, la relación es tan integral, única e igualitaria que resulta indiscernible.

Aunque podemos asumir que Dios es mucho más de lo que está sucediendo en el cosmos, basta con saber que el lugar donde Dios existe en la Tierra es tan personal como cada latido de nuestro corazón, pues nosotros somos la encarnación externa y visible de la divinidad. Somos la forma física, imbuida en el concepto del yo, que niega que seamos Dios a la vez que existimos con el único propósito de que *seamos uno*. Y, al ser uno, Dios siente en primera persona la realidad que creamos

Así que la mañana siguiente me desperté con la sensación de que tenía que asimilar lo que se me había explicado en el sueño para no volver a caer en el pensamiento (desde un punto de vista terrenal) de que Dios es algo distinto de todo y de todos, y empezar a cuestionarme después si está involucrado personalmente en las cosas horribles que ocurren o si se preocupa lo suficiente por evitarlas. Pido perdón por volver a caer en la redundancia: si algo puede suceder, sin importar lo espantoso e injusto o lo maravilloso y positivo que sea, es posible que suceda.

Es posible que suceda porque Dios se manifiesta a través de nosotros —y de toda la naturaleza— para experimentar todo lo que puede pasar (tanto lo bueno como lo malo), en nuestros términos, y todo lo que hay en medio; por consiguiente, nosotros y todo lo demás hemos sido creados y existimos para ese fin. Y puesto que es la experiencia de Dios, es también nuestra experiencia, no al revés. Por eso, Dios no podría ser más personal y, con todo, no parece ser personal en lo más mínimo, algo que resulta desconcertante. Ni siquiera parece existir en ese sentido.

Antes del sueño nada de esto se me había pasado por la cabeza. A colación de no apreciar el bosque entre los árboles, durante años me ha atraído el dicho «si no puedes ver a Dios en todo, no lo puedes ver en nada». Nunca lo había entendido bien hasta ahora. Gracias al sueño esta frase despierta en mí una *conciencia sagrada* que me deja sin aliento.

Epílogo

Somos uno es una percepción que he cultivado desde que tuve el sueño en 2010: supuso un cambio de conciencia que ha sido totalmente impresionante, sagrado y transformador para mí. Reconocer a Dios como uno mismo (y como otros) en lugar de verlo como una fuerza invisible, externa y creativa (separada de nosotros) requiere la evolución del propio espíritu y una profundización en la conexión propia Dios/alma a través de nuevas percepciones espirituales, sensibilidad e intuición. Abre el camino a una nueva forma de ser a través de una manera totalmente nueva de ver. Ahora veo claramente un mundo en el que no sucede nada que no sea la maravillosa realidad de que *Somos uno.*

«Somos uno» es ver, como aquel que ve, a través de los ojos de Dios.

ÊTRE NOUS (BEING US)
La perception de Dieu selon une vision radicalement différente

Être nous est dédié à l'élévation de l'esprit de la conscience et de la compréhension de la présence de Dieu dans nos vies.

« *Combien plus personnel peut être Dieu, si, en fait, l'expérience que j'ai, Dieu l'a – non pas en plus de moi, non pas avec moi, non pas à travers moi, mais en ayant exactement ce que j'ai, quand je l'ai – parce que nous sommes un et le même dans le temps et dans l'espace ?* »

Vous êtes-vous déjà demandé pourquoi des choses horribles arrivent ? Ou avez-vous remis en question l'existence d'un Dieu personnel ? Après la mort tragique d'une amie proche de sa fille, Lewis Randa a fait un rêve qui a changé sa vie et sa compréhension de l'existence de Dieu. Dans *Être nous (Being Us)*, Lewis réfléchit à ce qu'il décrit comme une nuit noire de l'âme et partage une révélation étonnante sur le rôle de Dieu dans nos vies – une révélation qui diffère grandement du récit promu par les grandes religions du monde. Lewis trouve un terrain d'entente avec le bouddhisme et la philosophie orientale, et il décrit comment il a adopté la doctrine du panenthéisme. Provoquant la réflexion et très instructif, *Être nous (Being Us)* présente un message édifiant qui plaira à toute personne ayant une grande ouverture d'esprit, un sens profond de l'émerveillement face à la création et la volonté de dépasser la pensée dualiste pour se sentir unie à Dieu.

PRÉFACE

Être nous (Being Us) est écrit dans un langage simple et conversationnel pour que son message soit accessible aux lecteurs de tous âges. Le format dans lequel les informations sont présentées et la mise en page générale sont conçus pour accompagner le lecteur dans l'assimilation progressive de perceptions qui peuvent être contraires à son éducation et à sa compréhension religieuses. Ce livre concis et sans prétention brise le concept patriarcal et dualiste de la divinité, non pas d'un point de vue ésotérique et théologique, mais simplement à travers un rêve, pendant une nuit noire de l'âme. S'il n'était pas question des enseignements religieux de la majorité des traditions religieuses au fil du temps, le message contenu dans ce livre serait intuitivement évident. Cette réflexion, espérons-le, causera une brèche dans l'armure de la pensée dualiste, surtout lorsqu'il s'agit de percevoir un Dieu personnel dans votre vie.

Faites attention à vos rêves, mes chers amis, car ils peuvent mener à une révélation qui changera votre vie. C'est le cas de ce rêve que je partage maintenant avec vous sous la forme d'un livre – un rêve qui a totalement bouleversé ma perception de Dieu. Il est traduit dans les principales langues des Nations unies, car son message est mondial – et son intention divine.

Sur votre chemin, gardez les yeux ouverts sur celui de Dieu en chaque personne et dans tout ce qui vous entoure. Il y a plus de Dieu dans votre vie que vous ne pouvez l'imaginer, plus qu'il n'y paraît, même lorsque vous avez vu la forêt à travers les arbres.

Lewis M. Randa

À propos de l'auteur :
Lewis Randa est un quaker, pacifiste, végétalien et militant pour le changement social. Il a fondé l'école The Life Experience School pour les enfants et les adultes handicapés en 1972, The Peace Abbey, un centre interconfessionnel pour l'étude et la pratique de la non-violence en 1988, et The Pacifist Memorial, un monument international qui commémore la vie des pacifistes en 1994. Son travail en faveur de la paix l'a conduit dans diverses régions du monde – du Salvador à Belfast, de Liverpool à Calcutta, d'Assise à Guernica. Lewis et sa femme Meg, avec laquelle il administre ces organisations, ont trois enfants adultes, Christopher, Michael et Abigail, et un nombre croissant de petits-enfants. Ils vivent dans la ville de Duxbury, sur le littoral du Massachusetts.

ÊTRE NOUS (BEING US)

Les rêves peuvent avoir l'effet le plus étonnant sur les gens, mais pour être honnête, je me souviens rarement des rêves assez longtemps pour les considérer comme étant tellement importants. Toutefois, il y a un rêve auquel je ne peux m'empêcher de penser et qui a changé ma façon de voir la réalité. Personne ne sait combien de temps la substance de ce rêve continuera à imprégner mon esprit et mon âme. J'espère que cela continuera pendant tout le reste de ma vie.

Lors de chaque nouvelle tragique et horrible de ces jours-ci, et il y en a eu beaucoup, je me suis posé la question que d'innombrables autres personnes se posent également, à savoir : comment peut-il y avoir un Dieu « personnel » ?

Avec toute la souffrance dans le monde – la famine, la pauvreté, l'indifférence, la violence, la guerre et les maladies – comment un Dieu personnel pourrait-il permettre que ces choses se produisent, étant donné que Dieu, apparemment, est aux commandes.

Le libre arbitre est une chose ; une tragédie insensée en est une autre. Après mûre réflexion, j'en suis venu à la conclusion que l'existence d'un Dieu personnel n'est qu'une idée réconfortante et pleine d'espoir que j'ai apprise au catéchisme. Mais à la lumière de toutes les tragédies et souffrances qui nous entourent, il semblerait que ce ne soit pas le cas. Ou, s'il y a un Dieu personnel qui permettrait à ces choses d'arriver à n'importe qui à n'importe quel moment, alors je suis certain de manquer quelque chose.

Puis une nuit, la nuit de Noël, à travers un rêve, ce que je ne comprenais pas m'a été expliqué.

Je suis allé me coucher après avoir passé un merveilleux Noël 2010 avec ma famille. Notre rituel pour les fêtes comprenait la récitation des prières pour la paix des principales traditions religieuses dans la chapelle interconfessionnelle de The Peace Abbey. Bien que troublé par la récente mort tragique d'une amie de ma fille, j'étais en paix, du moins avec le principe selon lequel toutes les personnes et toutes les choses qui existent sont une expression ou une création d'un Dieu d'amour et de bonté.

Ce qui me posait problème, cependant, c'était que ce soi-disant Dieu d'amour et de bonté permette que des choses aussi horribles se produisent de façon si aléatoire dans le monde. Il ne fait aucun doute que cette idée a traversé l'esprit de presque tout le monde à un moment ou à un autre, qu'il y a été répondu d'une manière ou d'une autre jusqu'à ce qu'elle ait dû être abordée à nouveau, dans des circonstances nouvelles, différentes et difficiles.

Ce que je n'avais pas compris, jusqu'à ce que cela me soit révélé dans le rêve, c'est que Dieu, avec qui j'ai remis en question une relation personnelle, vit réellement ce que nous vivons – physiquement, émotionnellement et mentalement, avec chaque expérience, partout et à tout moment, et c'est pourquoi toutes ces sortes de choses peuvent se produire. Dieu ne permet pas seulement que ces sortes de choses nous arrivent, Dieu permet que ces sortes de choses lui arrivent à lui aussi.

Le rêve m'a permis de prendre conscience du fait que tout ce qui peut se produire dans notre existence terrestre vaut la peine de se produire, aussi joyeux ou tragique que cela puisse être, parce qu'à travers ces expériences, Dieu arrive à se connaître lui-même en faisant l'expérience de toute la douleur, tout comme nous, de toute la joie, tout comme nous, de toute la peine et du chagrin, tout comme nous, et quand nous vivons ces expériences. Et ceci, dit le rêve, c'est parce que tout ce qui existe *est* Dieu. Rien de ce qui existe ne se produit en dehors de Dieu.

Il semble qu'en naissant dans un corps physique, et en succombant à des phases continues de développement du moi, nous nous détachons, non seulement de notre connexion avec Dieu, mais plus précisément, de la conscience que *nous sommes Dieu*, que tout ce qui nous entoure *est Dieu*, et que chaque expérience que nous vivons (ceci mérite d'être répété) est fondamentalement *une expérience de Dieu*.

Cette pensée ne m'avait jamais effleuré. Je ressentais que tout était sous le contrôle de Dieu dans un sens macro-universel, mais je n'avais jamais été près de considérer que Dieu avait mes expériences personnelles. Cela change tout. Je sens que je dois maintenant relire chaque texte important et significatif, chaque Écriture, chaque poème et chaque prière, et réétudier chaque philosophie, idéologie, théorie et principe de vie sur lesquels j'ai basé ma compréhension. Ce rêve a été pour moi l'élément déclencheur de tous les changements de paradigme.

Ce que Dieu est sur terre a été clarifié pour moi, en termes intimes, par ce rêve. Je reconnais maintenant, plus que jamais, que l'abandon du moi est nécessaire pour éclairer la conscience selon laquelle il existe un Dieu personnel auquel mon corps physique et ma personnalité donnent forme. Combien plus personnel peut être Dieu, si, en fait, l'expérience que j'ai, Dieu l'a lui aussi – non pas en plus de moi, non pas avec moi, non pas à travers moi, mais en ayant exactement ce que j'ai, quand je l'ai – parce que nous sommes un et le même dans le temps et dans l'espace ?

Dans l'existence terrestre, cette unicité a déconcerté l'humanité dans sa recherche de Dieu, car Dieu est caché dans le cadre du moi de la personne. Alors que le rêve me communiquait cette information, un sentiment de paix profonde et d'abandon de soi m'a enveloppé. Je me suis retrouvé dans un état de sommeil éveillé, sans images ni arrière-plan dont je me souviens. J'avais l'impression qu'on m'avait confié le secret de l'univers, que d'autres connaissent peut-être déjà, mais que je ne connaissais pas

Avant le rêve, je comprenais chaque expérience que je vivais comme étant la mienne. Comment pourrait-il en être autrement ? On m'avait appris que Dieu était *conscient* de toutes choses, même de mes expériences. On ne m'avait jamais enseigné, cependant, que Dieu *est* tout, et qu'il est donc *conscient* de tout ; et que Dieu est *conscient* de tout parce qu'il *fait l'expérience de* tout ! Nous pensons, en raison de notre séparation par rapport à ce que nous sommes réellement, que notre expérience personnelle n'appartient qu'à nous. Ce n'est pas ce que m'a appris mon rêve. C'est comme si, au réveil, j'avais vu Dieu dans tout ce qui m'entourait.

Maintenant, il semble que la question même, « existe-t-il un Dieu personnel ? » est semblable à une cellule de mon corps physique qui remettrait en question une relation personnelle avec moi parce que la cellule est incapable d'apprécier la relation entre nous. La relation, bien sûr, est tellement intégrale, tellement une seule et même chose, qu'elle est indiscernable.

Bien que nous puissions supposer que Dieu est bien plus que ce qui se passe dans le cosmos, il suffit de savoir que l'endroit où Dieu existe sur Terre est aussi personnel que chaque battement de notre cœur, car nous sommes l'incarnation extérieure et visible de la divinité. Nous sommes la forme physique, imprégnée d'un concept de soi, qui nie que nous soyons Dieu tout en existant dans le seul but que *Dieu soit nous*. Et en étant nous, Dieu vit à la première personne la réalité que nous créons.

Je me suis donc réveillé le lendemain matin avec le sentiment que ce qui m'avait été expliqué lors de ce rêve devait alors être assimilé pour que je ne tombe plus jamais dans l'idée (d'un point de vue terrestre) et que je commence ensuite à me demander si il ou elle est personnellement impliqué(e) ou si il ou elle se soucie suffisamment des êtres humains pour empêcher des choses horribles de se produire. Pardonnez la redondance une fois de plus : si quelque chose peut se produire, peu importe que ce soit horrible et injuste ou merveilleux et positif, cette chose peut se produire.

Elle peut se produire parce que Dieu se manifeste à travers nous, et à travers toute la nature, afin de faire l'expérience de tout ce qui peut se produire (à la fois le bon et le mauvais), dans nos termes, et tout ce qui se trouve entre les deux, et par conséquent, nous et tout le reste sommes créés et existons à cette fin. Et parce que c'est l'expérience de Dieu, c'est notre expérience aussi, et non l'inverse. Ainsi, Dieu ne pourrait pas être plus personnel, et en tant que tel, de manière mystifiante, il ne semble pas être personnel du tout. Ou même exister, d'ailleurs.

Avant le rêve, rien de tout cela ne m'avait traversé l'esprit. On parle de l'arbre qui cache la forêt. Pendant des années, j'ai été attiré par le dicton : Si tu ne peux pas voir Dieu en tout, tu ne peux pas voir Dieu du tout. Je ne l'avais jamais vraiment compris jusqu'à maintenant. Grâce au rêve, ce dicton m'éveille à une *conscience sacrée* qui me coupe le souffle.

Épilogue

Être nous (Being Us) est une prise de conscience que j'ai cultivée depuis que j'ai fait ce rêve en 2010 – ceci a entraîné un changement de conscience qui a été tout simplement impressionnant et sacré, et qui a changé ma vie. Reconnaître Dieu en nous-mêmes (et dans les autres), plutôt que de le considérer comme une force créatrice invisible et extérieure (séparée de nous), exige une évolution de l'esprit et un approfondissement de la connexion entre Dieu et l'âme par le biais de nouvelles perspectives spirituelles, de sensibilité et d'intuition. Cette reconnaissance ouvre une nouvelle façon d'être, à travers une toute nouvelle façon de voir. Je vois maintenant clairement un monde où il ne se passe rien qui ne soit pas la merveilleuse réalité de *Dieu étant nous*.

Être Nous (Being Us), c'est voir, comme celui qui voit, à travers les yeux de Dieu.

БОГ — ЭТО МЫ (BEING US)
Радикальный взгляд на восприятие Бога

«Бог — это мы» — книга, которая поможет вам лучше осознать и понять присутствие Бога в нашей жизни.

«Насколько ещё более персонифицированным может быть Бог, если на самом деле мой опыт — это опыт Бога? Не в дополнение к нему, не вместе с ним, не через него. Он переживает ровно то же, что и я, в тот же момент, потому что мы одно целое во времени и пространстве»

Вы когда-нибудь задумывались о причинах ужасных событий в нашей жизни? Сомневались ли в существовании персонифицированного Бога? После трагической смерти близкого друга дочери, Льюису Ранду (Lewis Randa) привиделся сон, который изменил его жизнь и представления о Боге. В книге «Бог — это мы» Льюис размышляет о «тёмной ночи души» и делится удивительным откровением о роли Бога в жизни каждого из нас, которое существенно отличается от догматов основных мировых религий. Льюис отмечает общие черты с буддизмом и восточной философией и рассказывает, как он пришёл к панентеизму. «Бог — это мы» — книга, дающая пищу для ума и озарение. Она несёт воодушевляющее послание, которое откликнется каждому, чей разум открыт для познания чуда мироздания. Она поможет выйти за пределы дуалистического мышления и прийти к осознанию единства с Богом.

ПРЕДИСЛОВИЕ

Книга «Бог — это мы» написана простым языком для того, чтобы её послание было доступно читателям всех возрастов. Материал подобран и представлен таким образом, чтобы читатель постепенно постигал идеи, которые могут противоречить его религиозному воспитанию или представлениям. Эта скромная книга позволит освободиться от оков патриархальной, дуалистической концепции божественности не с помощью эзотерического или теологического объяснения, а просто через сон, привидевшийся во время «тёмной ночи души». Если бы не учения большинства религий, насаждавшиеся нам много лет, послание этой книги было бы понятно интуитивно. Надеюсь, что представленные размышления позволят пробить брешь в незыблемой парадигме дуализма, особенно в том, что касается представлений о персонифицированном Боге в вашей жизни.

Друзья, обращайте внимание на свои сны, ведь они могут привести к прозрению, способному изменить вашу жизнь. Так произошло со мной, чем я и делюсь с вами в этой книге. Один из снов полностью перевернул мои представления о Боге. Книга переведена на основные языки Организации Объединенных Наций, так как её послание носит всеобщий характер, а замысел — божественен.

Следуя по своему пути, не упускайте возможности увидеть Бога во всех и во всём, что вас окружает. В вашей жизни больше Бога, чем вы можете себе представить — больше, чем станет доступно взору даже после того, как однажды за деревьями вы увидите лес.

Льюис М. Ранда

Об авторе

Льюис Ранда — квакер, пацифист, веган и общественный активист. В 1972 году основал школу «Жизненный опыт» (The Life Experience) для детей и взрослых с инвалидностью, в 1988 году — Аббатство мира (The Peace Abbey), межконфессиональный центр обучения ненасилию и его практики, а в 1994 году — Мемориал пацифистов (The Pacifist Memorial), международный памятник, посвященный миротворцам. Благодаря своей миротворческой деятельности Льюис Ранда смог побывать в самых дальних уголках мира: от Эль-Сальвадора до Белфаста, от Ливерпуля до Калькутты, от Ассизи до Герники. Вместе со своей женой Мег (Meg) он руководит перечисленными организациями. У них трое взрослых детей — Кристофер (Christopher), Майкл (Michael) и Эбигейл (Abigail) — и внуки, число которых растёт. Они живут в прибрежном городке Даксбери, штат Массачусетс, США.

БОГ — ЭТО МЫ (BEING US)

Сны могут оказывать на людей удивительный эффект. Но, честно говоря, они редко запоминаются настолько, чтобы считать их чем-то важным. И всё же об одном сне я не могу перестать думать. Он изменил мой взгляд на мир. Никто не знает, как долго его смысл сохранится в моей памяти и душе. Надеюсь, что он останется со мной на всю жизнь.

Каждый раз, когда я слышал о какой-нибудь трагичной и ужасной новости — а сегодня их предостаточно, — меня, как и многих других, начинал мучать вопрос: как может Бог быть «персонифицированным»?

В мире столько страданий — голод, бедность, безразличие, насилие, войны и болезни, — как же мог персонифицированный Бог допустить все эти беды, ведь считается, что именно Он за них в ответе.

Свободная воля — это одно, а бессмысленная трагедия — другое. После долгих размышлений я пришёл к выводу, что существование персонифицированного Бога — это лишь успокаивающая и дающая надежду идея, которой учат в катехизисе. Но на фоне всех трагедий и страданий, которые нас окружают, очевидно, что это не так. И всё же, если персонифицированный Бог существует и позволяет бедам случаться с кем угодно и когда угодно, то я определенно что-то упускаю.

Понимание того, что именно я упускал, пришло ко мне во сне одной рождественской ночью. В 2010 году, чудесно встретив Рождество в кругу семьи, я отправился спать. Обычно в этот день мы читали молитвы за мир всех основных религий в межконфессиональной часовне Аббатства мира. Я всё ещё переживал из-за недавней гибели друга дочери, но был в мирном расположении духа, по крайней мере принимал, что все и всё сущее есть выражение или порождение всемилостивого Бога.

И всё же я не мог понять одного: почему так называемый всемилостивый Бог позволяет подобным ужасам произвольно случаться в нашем мире? Наверняка почти каждому из нас в определённый момент жизни приходила в голову эта мысль. После долгих размышлений мы успокаиваемся, пока она снова не начинает тревожить нас, но уже при новых, иных обстоятельствах.

До тех пор, пока меня не озарило во сне, я никак не мог понять, что Бог, в существовании личной связи с которым я сомневался, в действительности переживает то же, что и мы — в физическом, эмоциональном и психологическом плане, с каждым нашим опытом, в любом месте и в любой момент времени. Именно потому всё происходит так, как происходит. Бог не позволяет событиям произойти с нами, он позволяет им случиться с собой.

Во сне я осознал, что все, что случается с нами во время земной жизни — и радостные события, и трагичные — происходит не напрасно: именно благодаря этому опыту Бог познает себя, испытывая ту же боль, ту же радость, то же горе, что и мы, одновременно с нами. Во сне ко мне пришло озарение: всё потому, что всё сущее *и есть Бог*. Ничто сущее не может не быть Им.

По всей видимости, в процессе рождения в физическом теле и прохождения через непрерывные этапы развития своего «Я», мы не столько теряем связь с Богом, сколько отстраняемся от осознания того, что *мы и есть Бог, всё вокруг есть Бог*, и каждый наш опыт (повторюсь) в основе своей есть не что иное, как *Бог, переживающий этот опыт*.

Эта мысль никогда ранее не приходила мне в голову. Я осознавал, что всё находилось во власти Бога во вселенском смысле, но никогда даже не мог подумать, что Бог проживает мой собственный опыт. Это изменило всё. Я почувствовал, что теперь мне нужно вновь прочесть все важные и значимые тексты, Священное Писание, стихи, молитвы и пересмотреть все философские взгляды, идеологии, теории и принципы жизни на которых основывалось моё миропонимание. Сон стал главным источником смены всех парадигм.

В уединении, во сне мне открылось то, чем является Бог на Земле. Теперь я больше, чем когда-либо понимаю, что прийти к осознанию персонифицированного Бога, которому мое физическое тело и личность дают форму, можно только усмирив свое эго. Насколько ещё более персонифицированным может быть Бог, если на самом деле мой опыт — это опыт Бога? Не в дополнение к нему, не вместе с ним, не через него. Он переживает ровно то же, что и я, в тот же момент, потому что мы одно целое во времени и пространстве.

В земной жизни это единство мешает человечеству в поисках Бога, так как Бог заключен в рамки индивидуальной личности. Когда эта идея пришла ко мне во сне, чувство глубокой умиротворенности и смирения охватило меня. Я обнаружил себя в состоянии сна наяву, не видел никаких образов, которые мог бы запомнить. Мне казалось, что я разгадал тайну мироздания, которая, быть может, была известна всем, но, определенно, не мне.

До этого сна я считал, что каждый свой опыт я переживаю в одиночестве. Да и как могло быть по-другому? Меня учили, что Бог *ведает* обо всем, что происходит, даже о моих переживаниях. Мне никогда не говорили, что Бог *и есть* всё, что происходит, и потому *знает* обо всем; и что Он *ведает* обо всём, потому что *переживает* всё, что происходит! Из-за отрыва от нашей истинной сущности мы полагаем, что наши личные переживания принадлежат лишь нам. Но мой сон опроверг это. На следующий день мне казалось, будто я начал видеть Бога во всех и во всём, что меня окружало

Теперь казалось, что сам вопрос «существует ли персонифицированный Бог?» стал сродни тому, как если бы клетка моего организма стала сомневаться в существовании личной связи со мной, потому что клетка неспособна оценить её. Ведь мы, безусловно, одно целое, и связаны так нераздельно, что границу различить невозможно.

Мы можем считать, что Бог гораздо больше всего, что происходит во Вселенной, но достаточно знать, что на Земле Бога можно ощутить так же близко, как биение сердца, ведь мы являемся внешним и видимым воплощением божественности. Мы – физическая форма, наполненная концепцией самости, которая отрицает тот факт, что мы и есть Бог, и одновременно существует лишь с единственной целью: *Бог – это мы*. Будучи нами, Бог от первого лица переживает реальность, которую мы создаём.

На следующее утро я проснулся с чувством, что открывшееся мне во сне теперь необходимо осознать, чтобы мне больше никогда не приходило в голову (с мирской точки зрения), что Бог — это нечто другое, не все и не всё, и чтобы я не начал опять задаваться вопросом, участвовал ли лично он/она/оно в ужасных событиях и сделал ли достаточно для того, чтобы не допустить их. Ещё раз повторюсь: если что-то происходит, каким бы ужасным и несправедливым или прекрасным и жизнеутверждающим оно ни было, ему позволено случиться.

Ему позволено случиться, потому что Бог проявляет себя через нас и через всю природу, чтобы пережить всё, что может произойти (как хорошее, так и плохое) в пределах нашего понимания. То есть мы и всё сущее созданы и существуем для этой цели. И поскольку это опыт Бога, это и наш опыт тоже, а не наоборот. Таким образом, Бог максимально персонифицирован и потому, загадочным образом, не представляется персонифицированным вовсе. Или даже не существует.

До того, как мне приснился сон, я ни о чем таком даже не думал. Говорят же, что «за деревьями не видно леса». На протяжении многих лет меня привлекало изречение: если вы не можете узреть Бога во всем, вы не можете узреть Бога вовсе. До этого момента я не понимал, о чем оно. Благодаря сну это изречение открыло мне *сакральное осознание*, захватывающее дух.

Эпилог

«Бог — это мы» — это осознание, которое я развивал с тех пор, как в 2010 году мне приснился описанный выше сон. Он дал толчок к изменению моего сознания. Это было сакраментальное и удивительное событие, изменившее мою жизнь. Для того чтобы принять Бога как самого себя (и как других), а не как незримую, внешнюю и созидательную силу (отдельную от нас), необходимо развивать собственный дух и углублять связь с собственным Богом/Душой с помощью новых духовных откровений, чуткости и интуиции. Тогда через этот совершенно новый взгляд на мир вам откроется иной способ бытия. Сейчас я ясно вижу мир, где не происходит ничего, что не было бы чудесным отражением того, что *Бог — это мы.*

Осознавать, что «Бог — это мы» значит видеть мир так, как это делает истинно зрячий: глазами Бога.

上帝即是我们 (BEING US)
感知上帝，有创见的洞察

《上帝即是我们》(BEING US) 倾力于提升对于"上帝存在于我们的生命中"这一灵性精神的认识和理解。

"如果上帝实际拥有与我相同的经历——不是附加，不是伴随，也不是以我为媒介，而是在我经历某件事情的同时与我拥有完全一致的经历——因为我们在时间和空间上皆为一体，那么上帝会在多大程度上更加充满个性？"

你是否曾想过为什么会发生可怕的事情？或者质疑是否存在人格上帝？路易斯·兰达 (Lewis Randa) 在他女儿的一位密友不幸去世后做了一场足以改变他人生的梦，让他改变了对上帝之存在的理解。在《上帝即是我们》(BEING US) 一书中，路易斯回忆了他所描述的灵魂的暗夜，并就上帝在我们生活中所扮演的角色分享了一个惊人的启示。这一启示与世界主要宗教所推崇的论述大相径庭。路易斯找到了佛教和东方哲学的共同点，并描述了他是如何接受泛神论教义。《上帝即是我们》(BEING US) 提出令人振奋的启示，发人深省，予人启迪。对于所有思维开放、对上帝造物怀有深深的好奇心、并愿意超越二元思维，接受与上帝融为一体的人而言，这本书具有广泛的吸引力。

前言

《上帝即是我们》(BEING US) 的语言风格朴素，言简意赅，娓娓道来，适合所有年龄段的读者阅读。内容格式和整体版面的设计颇为用心，使读者循序渐进地接受可能与其宗教教养和理解相反的观念。本书篇章紧凑，叙事温和，打破了宗法二元论的神性概念，它没有从深奥的神学角度出发，而是简单地通过灵魂暗夜中的一个梦来传达思想。如果没有长期以来大多数信仰传统的宗教教义，这本书中的启示显然不证自明。希望我们的反思能够打破二元思维禁锢，尤其是当你在生活中感知人格上帝的时候。

亲爱的朋友，请关注你的梦境，因为这可能会使你顿悟，从而改变你的人生。现在，我以书的形式与你分享这个梦——它颠覆了我对上帝的感知。本书凭借内容的全球性，以及神圣的目的，被翻译为联合国的多种主要语言。

在你前进的道路上，请留意身边的每一个人和每一件事，在其中发现上帝的存在。在生活中，上帝的存在超乎你的想象，即使你拥有窥一树而知全林的能力，上帝的存在也远远超出你的所见。

路易斯·兰达 (Lewis M. Randa)

关于作者

路易斯·兰达 (Lewis Randa) 是一位贵格会教徒、和平主义者、素食主义者和社会变革活动家。他于 1972 年创立了为残疾儿童和成年人服务的生活体验学校。1988 年创立了和平修道院，这是一家从事非暴力研究和实践的跨信仰中心。他还在 1994 年设立了纪念和平缔造者生命的国际纪念碑——和平主义者纪念碑。他积极推动和平事业，足迹遍及世界各地的偏远角落，从萨尔瓦多到贝尔法斯特，从利物浦到加尔各答，从阿西西到格尔尼卡。他和妻子梅格 (Meg) 一起管理这些组织，他们有三名成年子女：克里斯多夫 (Christopher)、迈克尔 (Michael) 和阿比盖尔 (Abigail)，还有越来越多的孙辈子女。 他们居住在马萨诸塞州的海滨小镇达克斯伯里。

上帝即是我们

梦境可以对人产生最惊人的影响，但老实说，我很少能长时间记住我的梦，因此并未觉得它们有多重要。然而，有一个梦让我无法停止思考，并且改变了我看待现实的方式。 谁都无法猜测这个梦的内容会在我的头脑和精神中持续多久。我希望能持续一生。

近日来不断传来的的每一条悲惨、可怕的消息都让我一直苦苦思索这个问题，这也是无数其他人苦苦思索的问题：怎么会有"人格"上帝呢？

面对世界上所有的苦难，包括饥荒、贫困、冷漠、暴力、战争和疾病，假设上帝掌管一切，人格上帝怎能允许这些事情发生。

出于自愿当然无可厚非，无谓的悲剧应另当别论。经过一段时间的深刻反思，我几乎得出了这样的结论：人格上帝的存在只是一个给人以希望和安慰的想法，这是我在教理问答中了解到的。 但是，从我们周围的所有悲剧和苦难来看，情况似乎并非如此。 或者，如果有一位人格上帝允许这些事情随时发生在任何人身上，那么我肯定遗漏了什么。

然后在一个圣诞夜，通过一个梦，我得到了解答。

2010 年，我与家人度过了美好的圣诞节后就去休息。我们的节日仪式包括在和平修道院不同宗教团体的小教堂里诵读主要信仰传统的和平祷文。尽管我女儿的一个朋友最近不幸去世，我感到难过，但我当时很平静，至少我相信存在的每个人和每件事都是慈爱的上帝的表达或创造。

然而，让我苦苦挣扎的是，这位所谓慈爱的上帝竟然允许如此可怕的事情在这个世界上随意发生。 毫无疑问，几乎每个人都在某个时刻产生过这样的想法，但人们只是在面对截然不同、充满困境的新情况下，且不得不再次应对它的时候，才会努力寻找答案。

直到这场梦为我揭示了我未能理解的东西，即上帝（我对与上帝的个人关系存在质疑）实际经历了我们所经历的一切，无论在身体、情绪和精神上，无论何时何地的每一次经历，这就是为什么上帝允许所有的事情发生的原因。上帝不仅允许事情发生在我们身上，上帝也允许事情发生在自己身上。

这个梦让我意识到，任何可能发生在我们尘世中的事情都是值得发生的，无论快乐的还是悲惨的，因为借由这些经历，上帝可以像我们一样通过经历所有的痛苦、快乐、悲伤和悲痛来认识自己：在我们这样做的时候，上帝同样也在这样做。这就是这个梦要告诉我的事情，究其原因，是因为存在的一切*都*是上帝。 存在者必然存在。

似乎在肉体诞生并屈服于自我发展的持续过程中，我们变得超脱，不仅是与上帝的联系，更准确地说，是意识到*我们即是上帝*，以及我们周围的一切*皆是上帝*，我们所拥有的每一次经历，（再强调一遍）从根本上说，都是*上帝在经历*。

我之前从来没有这样想过。我意识到在宏观普遍意义上，一切都在上帝的掌控之下，但从来没有想过上帝拥有我个人的经历。这改变了一切。我觉得我现在需要重读每一篇重要且有意义的文字、经文、诗歌、祷词，并重新审视我理解的每一种哲学体系、意识形态、理论和生活原则。对我来说，梦境是所有范式转变的根本来源。

这个梦为我详细阐明了上帝到底是什么。 我现在比以往任何时候都更加明白，一个人必须放弃自我，才能洞察这样一种意识，即确实存在一位人格上帝，并由我的身体和人格赋予其形态。如果上帝实际拥有与我相同的经历——不是附加，不是伴随，也不是以我为媒介，而是在我经历某件事情的同时与我拥有完全一致的经历——因为我们在时间和空间上皆为一体，那么上帝会在多大程度上更加充满个性？

在尘世中，这种一体性使人类在寻找上帝时感到困惑，因为上帝隐藏在人格的自我框架中。当我通过梦境得知这一切时，一种深刻的平静和臣服感包围了我。我发现自己处于一种警觉的睡眠状态，无法回忆起任何图像或背景。我觉得自己参悟了宇宙的奥秘，也许有其他人知道，但我之前肯定一无所知。

在做梦之前，我知道我的每一次经历都是我独自经历的。要不然还会有其他可能吗？我被教导说上帝*了解*所有事情，甚至我的经历。 然而，从来没有人告诉我，上帝*即是*万物，因此对万物都*了如指掌*；并且上帝*了解*所有事情，因为上帝正在*经历*所有事情！ 我们认为，由于脱离了真实的自我，个人经历就是我们自己的。但我的梦告诉我，并非如此。第二天，我仿佛从周围的每一个人和每一件事中都看见了上帝。

现在看来这正是问题所在，"是否存在人格上帝？"就像是我身体里的一个细胞在质疑与我的个人关系，因为这个细胞无法理解我们之间的关系。当然，这种关系是如此完整，如此统一，以至于难以区分。

我们也可以假设，上帝远不止存在于宇宙中发生的事情，但我们只需要知道上帝确实存在，并和我们一样具有人格，拥有每一次心跳，因为我们是神性的外在和可见的化身。我们是物质形态，充满了自我的概念，这一切立刻否认了"我们即是上帝"，而存在的唯一目的是 *上帝即是我们*。 在"上帝即是我们"的前提下，上帝以第一人称经历我们所创造的现实。

所以第二天早上醒来时，我意识到，我现在需要理解梦境向我传达的内容，这样我就再也不会陷入这样的思考（从世俗的角度），即上帝并不是每件事和每个人，然后开始质疑他/她/它是否亲自参与或足够关心我们，以防止可怕的事情发生。 请容许我再次赘述：如果有什么事情发生，无论它多么可怕、多么不公平、或多么美好、多么肯定，都是允许发生的。

之所以允许其发生，是因为上帝通过我们和一切自然事物让自己得以显现，以我们和其他一切事物的规则来经历一切可能发生的事情（包括好事和坏事）。因此，我们和其他一切事物都是为了这个目的而被创造和存在。因为这是上帝的经历，也是我们的经历，反之则不然。因此，上帝无疑是人格化的，也正因如此，才会令人费解，因为上帝看起来并非人格化。 甚至是为此而存在的。

在做这个梦之前，我从未有过这个念头。 不要只见树木不见森林。多年来，我一直对这句话深以为然：如果你看不见全部的上帝，你就根本看不见上帝。我直到现在才真正明白。 多亏了这个梦，让这句话唤醒了我的 *神圣意识*，这一意识令我震惊。

后记

《*上帝即是我们*》(Being Us) 是我自 2010 年那场梦境以来逐步形成的一种意识——它让我的认知发生转变，这可以说是令人敬畏的、神圣的转变，甚至可以改变人生。将上帝视为自己（和他人），而不是将上帝视为一种看不见的、外在的、创造性的力量（脱离我们自身），需要通过全新的精神洞察力、敏感性和直觉来使精神得以进化，加深个人与上帝/灵魂的联系。 它通过全新的观察角度开启了一种新的存在方式。 我现在清楚地看到了一个世界，在这个世界中的一切尽是*上帝即是我们*的奇妙的现实写照。

《*上帝即是我们*》(Being US) *通过上帝的眼睛看见一切，就如同我们看到的一样。*

For Arabic translation, begin from the last page of the book.

للترجمة العربية، إبدأ من آخر صفحة من الكتاب.

استيقظت إذاً في الصباح التالي مع شعور بأن ما شُرِحَ لي في حلم يجب أن أستوعبه الآن حتى لا يأخذني مجدداً التفكير (من وجهة نظر دنيوية) في أن الله شيء آخر غير كل شيء والجميع، ومن ثم أبدأ في التساؤل عما إذا كان هو/هي/هذا شخصياً معنياً أو مهتماً بما يكفي لمنع حدوث أمور مروعة. وسامحوني على التكرار: إذا كان يمكن أن يحدث أمر ما، مهما كان مروعاً وظالماً أو رائعاً ومؤكداً، فإنّه يُسمح بحدوثه.

يُسمح بحدوث هذا الأمر لأن الله يعلن عن نفسه من خلالنا، والطبيعة ككل، ليجرِّب كل ما يمكن أن يحدث (الجيد والسيئ)، بشروطنا، وكل ما بينهما، وعليه فإننا، نحن وكل شيء آخر، قد خُلِقنا ونحن موجودون لهذه الغاية. ولأن هذه هي تجربة الله، فإنها تجربتنا أيضاً، وليس العكس. لذلك لا يمكن أن يكون الله شخصياً أكثر، وهو على هذا النحو، وهذا أمر محيّر، لا يبدو شخصياً على الإطلاق، وحتى أنّ علة وجوده لا ترتبط بهذا الأمر.

قبل الحلم، لم يمرّ في ذهني أي من هذا، ولم أكن أدركه رغم تعمقي، وكنت لسنوات أميل إلى القول إنّه كنت عاجزاً عن رؤية الله في كل شيء، فلا يمكن رؤية الله البتة. ولم أفهم هذا الأمر إلّا الآن. وبفضل الحلم، أيقظ هذا القول فيّ معرفة مقدّسة تخطف أنفاسي.

الخاتمة

هو نحن معرفة طوّرتها منذ لحظة الحلم في عام 2010. فقد شكّل تحولاً في الوعي كان ملهمًا ومقدّسًا وقادرًا على تغيير الحياة. إنّ إدراك الله كمثل الذات (والآخرين)، في مقابل النظر إليه باعتباره قوة غير مرئية وخارجية وخلاقة (منفصلة عنا)، يتطلب تطوير الروح وتعميق العلاقة بين الله والروح من خلال رؤى روحية وتحسس وحدس جديد. فهذا يفتح مساراً كينونة جديد من خلال طريقة رؤية جديدة. والآن أرى أنا بوضوح عالماً لا يحصل فيه أي أمر خلاف الحقيقة المدهشة التي هي أن *الله هو نحن*.

هو نحن معناه أن نرى بعيون الله.

في الواقع هي نفسها تجربته – لا إضافةً عليها، ولا معها، ولا من خلالها، وإنما تجربتي أنا نفسها، عندما أخوضها – لأننا واحد ونحن نفسنا في الزمان والمكان؟

في الوجود الدنيوي، أربكت الوحدانية البشرية في بحثها عن الله، لأن الله يُخفى في إطار الأنا الشخصية. وبما أن ذلك كان يجري من خلال الحلم، فإن شعوراً بالسلام العميق والاستسلام الذاتي قد غلَّفني، ووجدت نفسي في حالة النوم المتيقظ دون صور أو خلفية يمكنني تذكرها. وقد شعرت وكأنني أُخبرت سرَّ الكون الذي ربما يكون الآخرون على علم به، ولكنَّني لم أكن بالتأكيد أعلم به.

قبل الحلم، كنت أفهم كل تجربة أمرّ بها وكأنها تجربتي الخاصة وحدي. ولكن كيف قد يكون الأمر غير ذلك؟ لقد عُلِّمت أن الله كان مدركًا لكل شيء، حتى تجاربي. لكنَّني لم أعلَّم أن الله هو كل شيء، وهو تالياً مدركٌ لكل شيء؛ وهو يدرك كل شيء لأنه يختبر كل شيء! ونحن نعتقد، بسبب انفصالنا عما نحن عليه حقاً، بأنَّ تجربتنا الشخصية هي ملكنا وحدنا. إلا أنَّ حلمي أظهر لي خلاف ذلك. وكان الأمر كما لو أنَّني رأيت الله في اليوم التالي في كل شخص وكل شيء من حولي.

الآن يبدو وكأن السؤال ذاته "هل هناك إله شخصي؟" هو أقرب إلى خلية على جسدي المادي تشكك في علاقة شخصية معي لأن الخلية عاجزة على تقدير العلاقة بيننا. والعلاقة بطبيعة الحال متكاملة وواحدة وهي نفسها لدرجة يتعذَّر تمييزها.

بينما يمكننا أن نفترض أن الله أكثر بكثير مما يحدث في الكون، يكفي أن نعرف أنه حيث الله موجود على الأرض فهو شخصي مثل كل دقة من دقات قلبنا، لأننا التجسيد الخارجي والمرئي للألوهيّة. فنحن الشكل المادي المشبّع بمفهوم للذات يقوم في آنٍ معاً بنكران بأننا الله، فيما علة وجوده الوحيدة هي أن *الله هو نحن*. وفي كوننا نحن، يختبر الله في الشخص الأول الواقع الذي نخلقه.

غير أن مصدر معاناتي كان أن هذا المُسمى إلهاً محباً يسمح بحدوث هذه الأمور المروعة بهذا الشكل العشوائي في العالم. ومما لا شك فيه أن الجميع تقريباً قد فكروا في هذا الأمر في وقت ما ليتجاوزوه ويعودوا إليه ثانيةً في ضوء ظروف جديدة ومختلفة وصعبة.

إنَّ ما عجزت عن فهمه، حتى كُشِفَ لي في الحلم، هو أن الله الذي شككت في علاقة شخصية معه، يختبر في الواقع ما نختبره – جسدياً وعاطفياً وعقلياً، مع كل تجربة في كل مكان، وفي كل الأوقات، ولذلك يُسمح بحدوث كل الأمور. فالله لا يسمح بحدوث الأمور لنا، بل يسمح بحدوثها لنفسه.

لقد جعلني الحلم أدرك أنَّ كل ما يمكن أن يحدث في وجودنا الأرضي يستحق أن يحدث، مهما كان مبهجاً أو مأساوياً، لأنه من خلال هذه التجارب يعرف الله نفسه باختباره كل الألم، تماماً كما نفعل، وكل الفرح، تماماً كما نفعل، وكل الحزن والأسى، تماماً كما نفعل، وعندما نفعل ذلك. وما جعلني الحلم أفهمه هو لأن كل ما هو موجود هو الله. وهو لا يغيب عن أي شيء موجود.

يبدو أنَّه في عملية الولادة في جسد مادي، ومع مرورنا بمراحل مستمرة من تطور الأنا، أصبحنا منفصلين، ليس عن علاقتنا مع الله فحسب، وإنما بشكل أدق عن إدراكنا بأنَّنا *الله*، وبأن كل شيء من حولنا هو *الله*، وكل تجربة نمر بها (وهذا أمر يستحق التكرار) هي بشكل أساسي *تجربةٍ يمر بها الله نفسه*.

لم أفكر بهذه الطريقة قطّ. وقد شعرت أن كل أمر كان تحت سيطرة الله بالمعنى الشامل، ولكنني لم أوشك قط على اعتبار أن الله يمرَّ بتجاربي الشخصية. وهذا ما يغيّر كل شيء. أنا أشعر الآن أنَّه عليّ إعادة قراءة كل نص وكتاب وقصيدة وصلاة مهمة وهادفة، وإعادة النظر في كل فلسفة وأيديولوجية ونظرية ومبدأ حياة بنيت فهمي على أساسه. لقد كان الحلم بالنسبة إليّ أساس كل تحولاتي الفكرية.

لقد توضّح لي ما هو الله على الأرض بعبارات حميمة بواسطة الحلم. وأنا الآن أدرك أكثر من أي وقت مضى أن التخلّي عن الأنا ضروري لتعزيز المعرفة بوجود إله شخصي هو مصدر جسدي المادي وشخصيتي. إلى أي عمق شخصي يمكن أن يصل الله أكثر إذا كانت تجربتي

(Memorial)، وهو معلم دولي لتكريم صناع السلام في عام 1994. وبحكم عمله في مجال السلام، جال في كل أصقاع الأرض، من السلفادور إلى بلفاست، ومن ليفربول إلى كلكتا، ومن أسيزي إلى غيرنيكا. وأنجب هو وزوجته ميغ التي تعاونه في إدارة هذه المنظمات ثلاثة أولاد هم كريستوفر ومايكل وأبيغيل، ولديهما عدد متزايد من الأحفاد. ويعيش الزوجان في بلدة دوكسبيري الساحلية في ولاية ماساتشوستس.

هو نحن

يمكن أن يكون للأحلام تأثير مذهل على الأشخاص، ولكن بصراحة، نادراً ما أتذكر الأحلام لفترة كافية لآخذ أي منها على قدر من الأهمية. بيد أنّ ثمة حلم واحد لا أستطيع التوقف عن التفكير فيه وقد غيّر الطريقة التي أرى بها الواقع. ولكن إلى متى قد يسود عقلي وروحي مضمون هذا الحلم؟ آمل في أن يسودهما مدى الحياة.

مع كل خبر مأساوي ومروع هذه الأيام، على كثرتها، كنت أواجه السؤال الذي يواجهه كثيرون أيضاً، ألا وهو كيف يمكن أن يكون هناك إله "شخصي"؟

مع كل المعاناة في العالم – المجاعة والفقر واللامبالاة والعنف والحرب والمرض – كيف يمكن أن يسمح إله شخصي بحدوث هذه الأمور، بما أنه يُفترض أن الله يتحكم بها.

تختلف الإرادة الحرة عن المأساة الفارغة من المعنى. وقد توصّلت إلى استنتاجات، بعد تفكير كثيف مع مرور الوقت، مفادها أنّ وجود إله شخصي ليس إلا فكرة مشجعة ومريحة أخذتها من التعليم المسيحي. لكن في ضوء كل المأساة والمعاناة من حولنا، لا يبدو أن هذه هي الحال فعلاً. أو إذا كان هناك إله شخصي يسمح بحدوث كل هذه الأمور لأي شخص في أي وقت، فأنا متأكد إذاً بأنّ شيئاً ما قد فاتني.

ثم في إحدى الليالي، في ليلة عيد الميلاد، أوضح لي حلم راودني ما فاتني.

تقاعدت بعد يوم عيد ميلاد رائع في عام 2010 مع عائلتي. وشملت طقوس عطلتنا تلاوة الصلوات من أجل السلام المستقاة من التقاليد الإيمانية الرئيسية في الكنيسة المتعددة المذاهب في دير السلام. ورغم اضطرابي بسبب الوفاة المأساوية لأحد أصدقاء ابنتي المقرّبين، إلا أنني كنت في سلام، انطلاقاً على الأقل من المبدأ القائل إنّ كل شخص وكل شيء موجود هو تعبير إله محب أو خلقه.

هو نحن كُتِبَ بلغة بسيطة وسهلة حتى يفهم القراء من جميع الأعمار الرسالة التي يحملها. وصُمِّمَت المواد والإطار العام لمواكبة القارئ بشكل يسمح له بالاستيعاب التدريجي لمفاهيم قد تتعارض مع تنشئته وفهمه الدينيين. ويخترق هذا الكتاب المقتضب والمتواضع من حيث الشكل المفهوم الأبوي والثنائي للإله، ليس من وجهة نظر باطنية ولاهوتية، بل ببساطة عبر حلم خلال ليلة مظلمة عبرت بها الروح. ولولا التعاليم الدينية لغالبية التقاليد الإيمانية عبر الزمن، لكانت الرسالة في هذا الكتاب بديهية بشكل طبيعي. ويُؤمل في أن يؤدي هذا التفكير إلى إحداث ثغرة في درع التفكير الثنائي، خصوصاً عندما يتعلق الأمر بإدراك وجود إله شخصي في حياتكم.

انتبهوا إلى أحلامكم، أيها الأصدقاء الأعزاء، لأنّها قد تؤدي إلى فهم عميق من شأنه تغيير حياتكم. وهذه حال الحلم الذي أتناوله في هذا الكتاب – وهو حلم خاص بمفهومي لله وقد حوّله رأساً على عقب. وتتم ترجمة الكتاب إلى اللغات الرئيسية للأمم المتحدة لأن رسالته عالمية وقصده إلهي.

وأنتم تسيرون في طريقكم، افتحوا عينيكم فترون الله في كل شخص وكل شيء من حولكم. وإنّ الله متغلغل في حياتكم أكثر مما قد تتخيّلون – أكثر مما تراه العين حتى وإن أمعنتم في التحديق.

لويس م. راندا

عن الكاتب:

لويس راندا ناشط سلمي ونباتي وفي مجال التغيير الاجتماعي ينتمي إلى جماعة الكويكر. وقد أسس مدرسة تجربة الحياة (The Life Experience School) للأطفال والبالغين ذوي الإعاقة في عام 1972، ودير السلام (The Peace Abbey)، وهو مركز متعدد المذاهب لدراسة اللاعنف وممارسته في عام 1988، والنصب التذكاري للسلام (The Pacifist

هو نحن (BEING US)

نظرةٍ معمقة لفهم الله

"هو نحن" عمل مكرس لتعزيز روحية الوعي وفهم حضور الله في حياتنا.

"إلى أي عمق شخصي يمكن أن يصل الله أكثر إذا كانت تجربتي في الواقع هي نفسها تجربته –
لا إضافةً عليها، ولا معها، ولا من خلالها، وإنما تجربتي أنا نفسها، عندما أخوضها – لأننا واحد
ونحن نفسنا في الزمان والمكان؟"

هل تساءلتم يوماً عن سبب حدوث أمور مروعة؟ أو هل تساءلتم إن كان هناك إله شخصي؟
يختبر لويس راندا بعد الوفاة المأساوية لأحد أصدقاء ابنته المقرّبين حلماً بدّل حياته وغيّر فهمه
في شأن وجود الله. في "هو نحن"، يسلّط لويس الضوء على ما يصفه بليلة الروح المظلمة،
ويتحدث عن إلهام مذهل حول دور الله في حياتنا – وهو دور يختلف إلى حد كبير عمّا تروج له
الديانات الكبرى في العالم. ويجد لويس أرضية مشتركة مع البوذية والفلسفة الشرقية ويصف كيف
اعتنق مذهب الحلولية. ويحمل الكتاب، المستفز للفكر والتنويري، رسالةً ملهمةً قادرةً على
استقطاب كل صاحب عقل منفتح، وإحساس عميق بالذهول بالنسبة إلى الخلق، ورغبة في
الارتقاء إلى ما هو أبعد من التفكير الاثنيني وبلوغ إحساس بالوحدانية مع الله.